George Salmon

A Sermon preached in St. Stephen's Church, Dublin

SALZWASSER
VERLAG

George Salmon

A Sermon preached in St. Stephen's Church, Dublin

Reprint of the original, first published in 1859.

1st Edition 2022　|　ISBN: 978-3-37512-854-8

Verlag (Publisher): Salzwasser Verlag GmbH, Zeilweg 44, 60439 Frankfurt, Deutschland
Vertretungsberechtigt (Authorized to represent): E. Roepke, Zeilweg 44, 60439 Frankfurt, Deutschland
Druck (Print): Books on Demand GmbH, In de Tarpen 42, 22848 Norderstedt, Deutschland

THE EVIDENCES OF THE WORK OF THE HOLY SPIRIT.

A SERMON

PREACHED IN

ST. STEPHEN'S CHURCH, DUBLIN,

ON SUNDAY, JULY 3, 1859,

BY

GEORGE SALMON, D.D.,
Fellow of Trinity College, Dublin,

WITH AN APPENDIX ON THE REVIVAL MOVEMENT IN THE NORTH OF IRELAND.

Third Edition,

WITH ADDITIONAL NOTES.

DUBLIN:
HODGES, SMITH, & CO., 104, GRAFTON-STREET,
Booksellers to the University.

1859.

A SERMON,

ETC., ETC.

---

1 JOHN iii. 24.

"And he that keepeth His commandments dwelleth in Him and He in him. And hereby we know that He abideth in us, by His Spirit, which He hath given us."

THESE are the concluding words of the Epistle for this day. Almost the opening words are, "*we know* that we have passed from death unto life, because we love the brethren." Again, in the middle of the Epistle we have, "My little children, let us not love in word, neither in tongue, but in deed and in truth ; and *hereby we know* that we are of the truth, and shall assure our hearts before Him." The subject then suggested by this oft-repeated "we know," and "hereby we know," is "the evidence of our state before God."

Immense is the change which every one who does not choose to pass sentence of condemnation on himself must trust and believe has taken place in him. The Apostle describes it in the emphatic words, we have passed *from death unto life.* A dead man is incapable of the actions of a living man: is insensi-

A 2

ble to the objects which give the living man pain or
pleasure: the dead body has within it no principle of
growth or of self restoration, but must fall away into
decay and corruption : so if we had leisure to deve-
lop the analogy, and to insist, for instance, on these
three points—incapacity of action, insensibility,
destiny to corruption—we might see how completely the word death expresses the condition of
those who are by nature born in sin and the
children of wrath. And as for children of grace,
who feel within themselves new power—strength to
do that of which they had been incapable before—
new thoughts, new emotions, new pleasures ; and
who know besides that all these bear with them
the promise of immortality ; *they* feel that the word
life is only adequate to express the change which
has taken place in their condition. Just as the life
of a vegetable deserves not the name of life, in
comparison with animal life—just as the life of a
beast deserves not the name of life in comparison
with that of him who is blessed with the gift of
reason; so, our animal and rational life is not
worthy to be called life, if we are not in possession
of that higher faculty which can ascend above the
things of sense and time—which can recognise the
God in whom we live, and move, and have our
being—and which can bring us into living union
with Him. There can, then, be no more important

question for each one of us than, do we bear about
in us the principle of that life, whose duration is
eternity ? Is it already working in us, and does it
prove its reality by its fruits ? What evidence can
be produced which will secure us from the danger
of mistake or self deception ?

In the text the proof relied on is " Hereby
we know that He abideth in us by the Spirit
which He hath given us." But he goes on immediately to say, (in a verse which, in our divi-
sion of chapters, is separated from the text, but
which is in close connection with it,) " Beloved,
believe not every spirit, but try the spirits,
whether they are of God, because many false
prophets are gone out into the world." He gives us
then further tests, viz. :—first, right faith : " Every
spirit that confesseth that Jesus Christ is come in
the flesh is of God ; and every spirit that confesseth
not that Jesus Christ is come in the flesh, is not of
God." Secondly, such works as are the fruits of
right faith, as we read in the words before the text
" He that keepeth His commandments dwelleth in
Him and He in him." And chief among these
commandments, the great commandment of love,
as I read before, " Hereby we know that we have
passed from death into life, *because we love the
brethren.*"

Now, brethren, we who had, three Sundays

ago, brought under our special consideration
the work of the third person of the Holy
Trinity—the blessed Spirit of God—all profess
to believe that our fitness to be partakers of
the inheritance of the Saints in light, depends
on our having been the subjects of His sancti-
fying grace.   It is a question then in which
we ought to feel a deep interest—what are the
ways in which the work of the Spirit manifests
itself—a question which we may be enabled to
answer from considering the tests given in this and
other passages of Scripture; may God bless the
consideration of it to us this day.

I must, then begin by cautioning you against
supposing that the work of the Holy Spirit
on the mind must necessarily be an object of
immediate consciousness on our part, or that it
is a work unaccompanied by work of ours.
From mistakes on this subject men, ever ready
to find excuses for doing what they like, have
sought in the doctrine concerning the work of the
Holy Ghost, an apology for their total neglect of
religion.   They imagine that they may continue
in sin until some future time, when it shall please
the Spirit of God, by some startling operation and
without any exertion of theirs, to make them on a
sudden holy and pure, and lovers of that which is
good.   Now, you must remember that the natural

operations of the mind are the workmanship of the same Spirit who breathed into our nostrils the breath of life; and those operations are not suspended, but rather restored to their freest exercise, when God, by His grace, regrants us that liberty of which the fall had deprived us. Since then the work of the Holy Ghost is not an interruption of the exercise of our natural faculties, but rather a harmonious development of them, it must become an object of consciousness, not directly but by its results. Rude and sudden changes usually mark the works of man, but the works of nature generally increase by gradual and scarcely perceptible transitions, which require the lapse of some time to make them remarkable. And it is among these that our Lord has sought an emblem for the work of grace in the heart when he compares it to the seed "which a man casts into the ground, and which, while he sleeps and rises night and day, springs and grows up he knows not how." Those, therefore, who neglect the ordinary means of grace, expecting some more violent exercise of God's power on their hearts, should reflect that what they look for is contrary to the analogy of the Divine proceedings, that their expectation is unsupported by any promise of God's Word, and that even if gratified, it would be of questionable advantage. The air which surrounds us is not less really present when in silent tranquillity it supplies all with the indispensable condition of existence, than when it more strikingly manifests itself in the howl of the storm, and the tumult of the hurricane. But men incur the danger, that while they seek for God in the whirlwind of emotion, where he is not, they refuse to listen to the still small voice of His Spirit. Beware then, lest while expecting the fruits of the Spirit to spring up suddenly in your souls, you should meanwhile allow that wicked one to snatch away the good seed already sown in your hearts. Just as at the time when the second person of the Trinity dwelt upon earth, the majority of those with, whom He sojourned, were unconscious of His presence ; they longed for the time when their deliverer should come ; and professed their belief, that when Messiah should come, he would show them all things ; and they looked eagerly for the sign from heaven which was to announce his triumphant advent. Yet, all the time, He whom they sought was among them, dispensing temporal and spiritual blessings, to all who were willing to lay aside their own prejudices, as to the manner in which they conceived their Redeemer should come, and who were willing to accept those blessings in the form in which it had pleased God to bestow them. And in precisely the same way may he who defers his repentance, in the expectation of receiving some future call from the Holy Ghost, be unconscious of the summons He has already given. The reproaches of your consciences for neglected opportunities—the convictions of sin forced on you sometimes by the Word of God, read or preached,— the lessons, it may be, taught you by God's afflictive dispensations—your occasional desires after greater holiness;—all these may be the strivings with you of that Spirit who is able to subdue Satan under your feet.

Further, the work of the Spirit in our hearts is not unaccompanied by exertion of ours. The Bible always represents the work of God's Spirit as a work done *on* the wills of His people. He is the source of all holy desires, all good counsels, all just works ; and yet it is not that He causes men, as senseless machines, to perform certain actions, but it is that he so shapes their wills that they, as rational voluntary agents, do those things which are pleasing in His sight. We are not carried to Heaven like inanimate objects, but we ourselves receive strength to tread by our own steps the way to Zion. We are ourselves the soldiers who are enabled by the might of that Spirit, to subdue our spiritual enemies. It is just as Canaan of old was bestowed on the Jewish people.—" They gained not the land in possession by their own sword, neither was it their own arm that helped them, but thy right hand, O Lord, and the light of thy countenance,' because thou hadst a favour unto them." But it was not that God sent a pestilence to sweep their enemies away—His destroying angels were not sent forth to scatter their foes ; it was on their own long-continued warfare that the blessing was bestowed. They were not allowed to leave any of their fighting men behind : the warriors of the two tribes and a half who got possessions on the other side of Jordan, were required to join their brethren in the conquest of Canaan ; they were allowed to neglect no military precautions which would be used by an army that relied on human strength alone. So it is that a sense of complete dependance on God as our only source of strength may be accompanied with the conviction that it is our duty to use at His command every power He has bestowed on us, as energetically as if we fancied the work was to be done by us alone.

I shall touch on another analogy which may illustrate the truth that the supernatural assistances bestowed by the Holy Spirit are compatible with a large amount of voluntary active exertion on the part of the human agent. I allude to the subject of the inspiration of the books of Scripture ; where, while we acknowledge the divine origin of all, yet the human element can be distinctly traced ; and we observe the same differences of style between the writings of St. John and St. Paul, for example, as if they had been the fruit of their unaided power. Just, then, as the extraordinary gifts of the Spirit poured on the apostles and evangelists, did not suspend the exercise of their intellectual powers, but were employed in directing and developing these powers according to the ordinary laws which regulate their exercise, so we may expect the ordinary gifts of the Spirit to be given in such a manner as not to interfere with the voluntary exercise and the natural development of the powers of him who is the subject of this spiritual influence.

The next thing that I wish you to observe is, that the Spirit's work is one on our whole nature. There is a work done *on our understanding*, enabling us to receive and confess the truth, under the teaching of Him who has been promised as our guide, to lead us into all the truth—who was to bring into the apostles' memory all that their Lord had said unto them, whose office it is to enlighten the eyes of our understanding, and to guard us against error as well as against sin. This is one part of His work alluded to in the beginning of the 4th chapter of this epistle of St. John. But there is a further work upon *the life and conduct*, enabling us to pro-

duce those good works in which it is ordained that
God's people should walk.   But this work is not
confined merely to the outward conduct ; it extends
also to the *inward affections* of the heart.   It is He
who produces in us those *thoughts and emotions*
which become one called of God.   It is He who
fills us with a love of God and of holy things.   It
is He who inspires us with a hatred of sin—it is He
who enables us to feel real sorrow for all our sins,
and real gratitude for the work of our redemption,
in which by the sacrifice of His own life, our
blessed Lord redeemed us from the curse.   All
these are parts of the Spirit's work which, as I said,
operates *on our entire nature*, and displays itself in
the harmonious development of all the parts of our
nature, and not by causing the distorted growth of
any one part, while all the rest is stunted and neglected.   This is just the difference between God's
way of working and man's.   It is unavoidable that
we should give our attention to but one thing at a
time, and even when the results of man's labours
are   the   most   harmonious   and   symmetrical,
these results are obtained by attending to each
part for a time, and leaving the rest for a time
neglected.   Thus we may contrast the process by
which the statuary proceeds, shaping each limb
successively into form, while the other parts are for
the time neglected, with the natural growth of

the living frame, in which all the parts together make harmonious increase. We can imitate the harmony of God's works, when we take care to give attention to each part in turn, but it often happens that we forget to do this, and that the particular work on which we are called on to labour engrosses our attention, and causes us to be forgetful of the rest.

So it is in religion. To its perfection these three things are necessary which I have mentioned —namely, right faith, good works, pious emotions. No one would be right who should deny the importance of any one of them; but yet it often happens that people have their minds so full of the importance of some one of the three, that they practically forget the rest, even if they do not in words deny the necessity of them. Thus, no one who believes in the Bible can deny the importance of right faith. We are, in fact, there taught, that God performed a series of most stupendous miracles in order to reveal certain truths to mankind. Who, then, that believes this, can count it as a matter of small importance whether or not mankind receive and believe them. If it were a matter of indifference, all these miracles would have been wrought, we may say, in vain. But then there are some so full of the importance of right belief, that they seem to think this everything. They have words of unsparing condemnation for those who differ from them in belief,* while they are ready with indulgence for the laxity and shortcomings of those whom they consider sound in doctrine. And in their own case they are in danger of being content with an accurate knowledge of doctrine as a substitute for Christian lively faith. And yet a man may have a perfect head knowledge of all the doctrines of the Christian faith—he may be able to defend our religion against all the objections of infidels, he may know thoroughly all the perversions of the truth that heretics have imagined, and may be able to expose and refute them all. He may understand all mysteries and all knowledge, and yet may lack the distinguishing temper of Christianity, that charity without which his knowledge can profit him nothing. The fact is, none of the doctrines of Christianity were revealed merely to gratify curiosity; they were made known to us because they all tend most strongly to influence our practice, and if our knowledge of them does not bear this fruit, such barren knowledge is possessed in vain.

Take next the second part of religion which I mentioned—good works; and I do not think I need waste time in saying a single word to point out its importance; because it must be admitted at once by those who value the Scriptures and those

* The word "miscreant," which is etymologically "misbeliever," is a remarkable instance of this, in its ordinary use.

who do not. Even those who care nothing about religion can appreciate morality, and can admire a holy, self-sacrificing life, even though they know nothing of the motives which have inspired such conduct. And no one who reads and believes his Bible can think lightly of holiness, or suppose that it is a matter of little moment whether believers show by their works that their faith is a living and not a dead one. But there are some persons who seem to think that religion is nothing more than a contrivance for securing external morality, and that provided this result is produced we need care for nothing else. These persons give hearty approval to the Christian preacher when he comes forward as the inculcator of secular morality, when he tells his people (as he ought to do), that their religion is valueless if it expend itself in talk, or if it be confined to the church, or. to the Sunday, and if it do not render them more faithful in the discharge of every duty of life ; and when he says that the doctrines of Christianity may do their work most effectually when they are not talked of. As long as religion is used in this way, as a means to an end, they can tolerate it, but not so when it intrudes itself any further. If they see persons strongly impressed with a sense of their sinfulness in the eyes of God, deeply grateful for the work of our Saviour's redemption, realising strongly, in short, that their existence is not to be limited by the bounds of this narrow world—then they have no patience with such irrational enthusiasm, as they consider it, and will probably set down all such feelings as delusion, or mania, or temporary insanity. If we keep strongly before us the fact that this world is intended by God to be our place of preparation, our training school for another, we shall be guarded against two opposite errors. We shall feel, on the one hand, that no system of religion can be right which leads us to neglect the ordinary duties of life, since these duties are the work which God has given us to do, knowing that the performance of them will form in us the habits and the character necessary for us hereafter : but we shall also feel that the cares and pleasures of this passing scene are not in themselves worthy to occupy all our thoughts. This place is not our home : our common work here may be the best preparation for our future existence, and so may fitly employ our best energies. But the thoughts of that future home, of that after existence, can never be out of place here ; we can never be wrong in fixing our thoughts on Him who is not only our guide through time, but who is to be our portion through eternity.

Thus, then, we have seen that neither right faith nor good works alone constitute religion, but neither do pious emotions of themselves make up the whole of religion. The importance of such feelings none can dispute. When we make confession of our sins, our hearts should also be humbled with a sense of our vileness. When we repeat acknowledgments to God for His mercies, it is necessary that our hearts should also expand in devout thanksgivings to God. When we read of the sacrifice of His Son, our hearts should also be filled with wonder and gratitude at the exceeding greatness of His love, who thus died and gave Himself for us. But if we possess such feelings, are we therefore safe ? Can we trust to them without danger as certain evi-dences of our spiritual health ? Alas, it is certain that we cannot. We are fearfully and wonderfully made, and it is extraordinary how much the power of exciting such feelings depends on the state of our bodies, our constitutional temperament, and our nervous susceptibility. What might make us sus-pect that these could not correspond exactly to our spiritual state, is that the tendency of such feelings is to become less vivid the oftener they are excited ; so that they do not grow with our growth in grace ; and the aged Christian may feel it impossible to experience the same raptures of love and wonder which filled his soul when first he learned to know that the Lord is gracious. Religious excite-ment—strong emotion, is a thing, which, from its nature, cannot be lasting. It is like the corn of wheat cast into the ground, whose nature it is to

decay and die ; but it may live in its permanent
effects, by producing the fruits of changed habits,
and new principles of action. Religious excitement
may be, and often is, a good thing. The tendency
to worldliness is so strong with us all ; we are so
prone to fix our whole thoughts on things below,
and to lose all power of realising the existence of
anything higher, that it does us good to be brought
into contact with others who are strongly impressed with the reality of eternal things, and so to
have our own feelings stirred up, and to be made
capable, in this way, of forming resolutions and
commencing plans from which, in cooler moments,
indolence or indifference might have kept us back.
Metal when heated may be made to take a form
with ease, which when cold it would stubbornly
have resisted. But then you will observe that the
essence of the whole thing is that it *does* take a
new form. The mere heating it and letting it cool
again can lead to no useful result. But this is the
mistake which many make about religious excitement. They look on it as *in itself* the good
result which it is desirable to produce, instead of
being the *means* which, by God's blessing, may be
the cause of a change of life. Many are taught to
look for the evidence that God has given them His
Spirit, not in his present work on their souls, but
in the fact that at some former time they have

been the subject of strong religious emotions. They are satisfied to know that the metal was once heated, instead of asking what form it assumed. And this plan of looking to the past instead of to the present, is productive at times of opposite evils. With some who think that if they ever have experienced certain emotions, they must be safe for ever, it may produce presumption and false security ; with others who feel themselves obliged to acknowledge that they are now incapable of reviving in themselves anything approaching to the feelings they once experienced, the temptation arises to believe that, having fallen away from grace, they have arrived at a state at which it is impossible to renew them to repentance.

In speaking of this subject of religious emotion it is right to make mention of the attempts that have recently been made in the North, and, with so much success, to produce such emotions extensively and violently.

And if I say something as to the natural causes of the success of such attempts, I must remind you that to speak of the natural causes of any thing does not exclude the agency of Him who is the great First Cause of all. For instance, those who think but little of the hand of God in the common events of life, have always been ready enough to recognise His hand in His unusual visitations, such as an earth-

quake or pestilence. Suppose, now, that with increased acquaintance with the laws of nature, we
are able to trace the natural causes of these also—
to find, for example, the sanitary laws by the
neglect of which pestilence is caused, do we then
shut out God from His world? No ; we only learn
more of Him by knowing the laws according to
which He works, but He remains the Great First
Cause of all. And if we learn also, as it is likely we
may, more of the laws according to which the body
acts on the mind, and according to which one
mind acts on the other, there is nothing atheistical
in such knowledge; for we must believe that all
these natural laws are directed and overruled by
God to execute His will.   To say that anything is
produced by natural causes, does not exclude it
from being the very means appointed by the
Spirit of God to do His will.   With this explanation as to what I mean by natural causes, I must
own my belief, that there is nothing which we
read of as taking place in the North which can
appear otherwise than as perfectly natural to any
one acquainted with the sympathetic influence of
emotion in large masses, and with the means by
which nervous susceptibility may be artificially
heightened. What may convince any one that
human means have a share in producing the results
of which I speak is, that those results do not be-

long exclusively to any one form of Christianity, but are to be found in those that differ most widely. In the revivals of America last year, the Unitarians had their share as well as those whose doctrines agree with ours.

And the person, perhaps, who best understood the art of exciting religious emotion, and who reduced it to a regular system, was the founder of the order of Jesuits. Any person who knows anything of the system of spiritual exercises which he invented, how the disciples in their retreats, assembled together in a darkened chapel, have their feelings worked up by ejaculations gradually lengthening into powerful descriptions, first, of the punishment due to sin, of the torments of hell and purgatory, then of the love of God, of the sufferings of the Saviour, the tenderness of the Virgin ; how the emotion, heightens as the leader of the meditation proceeds, and spreads by sympathetic contagion from one to the other :—any one who knows anything of this must be aware that the Roman Catholic Church has nothing to learn from anything which the most enthusiastic sects of Protestants have invented. The most violent and extensive religious excitement that history records took place in one of the darkest periods of the Church's history. I mean that which led to the Crusades ; when millions of Christians thoroughly believing what they exclaimed " it is the will of God"—deserted their homes only to perish in heaps in a foreign land. Who shall say that that movement* was all superstition and fanaticism ; for it was participated in by the best and the most devout of the time.   No doubt it was then blessed by God to the awakening and conversion of many a careless soul; and the sacrifices which they saw others make, and which, led by their example, they were themselves persuaded to make, in what they believed to be the cause of God, must have made them feel that religion was a real thing. But, yet, the result proved how much that great movement was brought about by merely human causes.   For we cannot believe that God seduced those great multitudes with false promises, and led them out to perish miserably in a distant land.   We see then that religious excitement may exist without religious knowledge.

A clerical friend of my own told me a day or two ago of a woman who had been " stricken down" in his neighbourhood, and who was pointed out by the Methodist preacher as a case of signal conversion.   And when my friend came to converse with her he found to his amazement that she was ignorant of the most elementary truths of the Gospel, and had merely an idea that the physical sufferings

* See a Sermon lately published by Rev. Richard Oulton on Religious Revivals.

she experienced during her " conversion" were in some way to atone for her sins.

Yet I have not the least doubt in the world that in many cases permanent fruits will remain of this movement. I believe that many who had been halting between two opinions before may be henceforth fixed in pursuing the right course which they have now openly chosen, that many may be now roused from a state of carelessness and indifference, and may under the influence of this excitement form resolutions which God's grace will enable them to keep, and may commence habits in which He will enable them to persevere. I could wish then that I had been able to speak in terms of entire and unqualified approval of a movement which may lead to such good results. For, no doubt, the evil we have most to contend with is the worldliness which prevails so generally, the habit so common with ourselves, and all about us of living and acting, as if this world were to be our home for ever. No wonder that good men are ready to welcome without too severe examination any thing which rouses men from their indifference to religion. But we must not do evil that good may come. It is the duty of a Christian minister to speak what he believes to be the truth, no matter how great the temptation to reserve it ; nay, even if it seemed to him that to keep it back would do God's work better. And I have faith to believe that he who does thus boldly speak the truth will find it in the end more expedient also, and more useful than any disguise of it could have been. Believing then, as I do, that many mistake bodily excitement produced by artificial means for the work of God's Spirit, it is my duty to say so plainly, even at the risk of seeming to discourage the efforts of pious men to promote the glory of God. God, I say, can bless this as well as He can cause all other things to work for good, and to promote the extension of His kingdom. When the cholera swept through these countries I have no doubt that the visitation was blessed by God to the souls of many who were thereby awakened to solemn thoughts of death and eternity, that had been strangers to their minds before. But would a knowledge of these good effects justify any one in introducing such an epidemic[*] into the country, even if he could be sure that it would in no case terminate fatally. And I consider it just as unlawful to produce artificially hysterical and nervous disease. Seasons of bodily depression are, no doubt, favourable to religious

---

[*] "The very phraseology of the people, in speaking of this great work as of some mysterious epidemic, spreading with resistless power from house to house, and bringing death to their old habits, and thoughts, and hopes, was to me not the least affecting part of my experience. 'She took it, and she was very bad with it.' 'Took what?' ' Oh, just the revival.' 'I have a brother and two sisters and none of us took it.' As the right focus in looking at a painting, an awe-struck reverential frame of soul in looking at these Irish revivals is indispensable."—*Letter of Rev. Duncan MacGregor, of Glasgow.*

thoughts, yet we have no right to throw peoples' bodies into an unhealthy state in the hope of saving their souls. And experience shows that if we were to do so, it would be very doubtful if we should produce permanent good effect. Every one knows how constantly the good resolutions formed in times of sickness and trial are dissipated by returning health and prosperity. The fact is, religious excitement is good, not for itself, but for what it may lead to; and the danger of it is that it is often succeeded by a reaction which leaves the subject of it in a more unfavourable condition than before.

I believe then that we may distinguish the Spirit's work from man's, in that it is a harmonious development of these three results, of which I have been speaking—right belief, good works, pious emotions. Its faith is not a mere barren speculative belief, not a mere repetition of orthodox formulas; its morality not the mere compliance with worldly proprieties, nor the mere observance of ordinary duties; its emotions not transient and barren excitement succeeded by deadness afterwards. But its love is founded on knowledge, and brings forth the fruits of righteousness.

And this work may not be the less real because it may proceed quietly and gradually, and because we cannot point to some sudden change as the epoch of its commencement. We might as well disbelieve what science tells us that the globe we inhabit is careering through space with a velocity which our imagination can scarcely conceive, because this motion does not make itself manifest to our senses, by noise and jolts and fitful interruptions, as the motions which we ourselves originate are accustomed to do.

One lesson, however, we may learn from the subject I have been speaking of. If any good results of this revival movement can be traced to the blessing of God bestowed on the use of human means, then the use of these means (as long as counterbalancing *evil* effects are not produced also) becomes a Christian duty. Foremost among the human agency which has been blessed for good, I place the power of sympathy ; by virtue of which when many are assembled together, emotions felt by several propagate themselves to the rest, intensifying as they spread. It is this power of sympathy which has in many places produced results which seem to be miraculous, and has stirred up the flames of emotion to a height that has perplexed those who witness it. On the other hand, what is it that chills and deadens similar feelings among ourselves so much as the fear, that if we express them we shall meet with no sympathy from those about us. So are we tempted to be ashamed of Christ ; to bury in silence, and, at last to stifle thoughts and feelings that we have no confidence will be responded to by those to whom we are inclined to express them. Yet if we really believed these truths which we profess to acknowledge, why should we doubt to strengthen each other's faith by each letting the other see that we do really think and act and feel as if the things we profess were true. Wherever this is done there are in such congregations not one or two preachers of God's Word, but many ; and we may expect a harvest of souls for Christ great in proportion to the additional number of labourers thus sent to work in His harvest.

I will conclude by reading you the special promise of God's blessing on the mutual intercourse of those that fear the Lord :—" Then they that feared the Lord spake often one to another, and the Lord hearkened and heard it, and a book of remembrance was written before him for them that feared the Lord and that thought upon his name. And they shall be mine, saith the Lord of Hosts, in that day when I make up my jewels, and I will spare them as a man spareth his own son that serveth him. Then shall ye return and discern between the righteous and the wicked, between him that serveth God and him that serveth him not."

APPENDIX.

I know that some pious men who have gone down to witness what has taken place in the North, have been carried away by what they saw ; and I can conceive that to some of them it may appear almost profane to ascribe, as I have done in the preceding sermon, a great part of that work to the use of human means ; nay, to the use of means which, injudiciously employed, may produce even mischievous results. To recur, however, to an illustration which I have already employed, I can conceive also that an uneducated person may contemplate with devout awe the tumult of a thunderstorm, believing that in the thunder he heard the very voice of God, and that in the lightning he saw the very hand of God stretched forth to smite in destruction ; and I can conceive that such a person might shrink back, as if from profanity, if he were told, "you behold but the operation of a mighty natural agent, of a power which man is capable of subduing to his own uses; which may, if rightly employed, be the means of bestowing signal blessings on mankind, but which, if tampered with indiscreetly, may cause the death of those who meddle with it." And yet we know that the philosopher who should tell him so would speak nothing but the truth, and that he might be withal as sincerely pious as the other, and might believe as firmly as the ignorant man that "it is the glorious God that maketh the thunder." If it is possible for us to learn anything of the laws of nature, that is to say of the rules according to which the great Author of nature works, there is nothing devout in remaining ignorant of it. If we ascribe the results of such natural laws to miracle, we do God no honour thereby, but we do ourselves the injury of losing whatever power to glorify God and to profit ourselves or our fellow-creatures a knowledge of those laws would have gained for us. And if our ignorance is wilful, do we not incur the condemnation of that " wicked and slothful " servant who left unimproved a talent which he might have employed for his master's benefit? Still more, if through wilful ignorance of these laws, we do injury to ourselves or our fellow-creatures, can such ignorance be regarded as else than sinful?

We have still much to learn as to the laws according to which the mind and body act on one another, and according to which one mind acts on another ; but it is certain that great part of this mutual action *can* be reduced to general laws, and that the more we know of such laws the greater our power to benefit others will be. If, when, through the operation of such laws surprising events take place, we cry out indolently like Turks, " Such is the will of God," instead of setting ourselves to inquire whether it was the will of God to give us power to bring about or to prevent these results, then our conduct is not piety but sinful laziness. I have no hesitation in saying that the sympathetic force which the emotions of a large assembly exert on individuals present is as really a mighty natural agent as the electricity of the thunder cloud ; that this power if wisely employed, may be made to produce most beneficial results, and if indiscreetly tampered with may produce most dangerous ones. Thus, in the history of the present movement, it has been stated in the newspapers, that several cases of mental derangement have occurred, including the case of one minister who took an active part in the movement.* I lay no stress on anonymous paragraphs, but I cannot refuse credence to the following extract from a letter which appeared in the *Daily Express*, signed W. Craig, and dated Limaherry, Ahoghill, and describing what the writer saw in his own locality, especially as the writer sympathizes strongly with the revival movement:—

"There is another side of the picture which I am almost afraid to turn to you, but I feel that I would not be doing my duty if I would keep it back. There are three or four persons in this locality who have not got better from their conviction, and are raving maniacs as yet. I cannot look upon them without shuddering. They seem to answer the description of those given in the New Testament as possessed of devils. This is, as I think, God's mysterious work, but I cannot fathom it."

Testimony to the same effect will be found at p. 54, from the Rev. Samuel Moore, of Ballymena, a leader in the Revival Movement.

The Rev. Mr. M'Ilwaine,† of Belfast, says—

"After a good deal of actual examination, I have to state my belief that there is a dangerous physical malady abroad, and that its seat is in the

---

* In reference to this case, Rev. Dr. Morgan, a Presbyterian Clergyman of Belfast, writes (*Saunders*, July 4), "What if some were deranged: How many were deranged by the failure of the Western Bank in Scotland? Are all, then, to have no more to do with banks? The absurdity of the conclusion is obvious." If pecuniary losses are sometimes followed by derangement of mind, I apprehend we may learn from it that it is a wrong thing to risk one's property in hazardous speculations of a gambling character. But we are not to condemn all banking because one bank fails, any more than we ought to condemn this revival movement, or any other movement, because one person in the course of it becomes deranged. If several such cases, however, occur, a case of strong suspicion arises that there must be something reprehensible in the management of it.

† In the First Edition I quoted a newspaper report of Mr. M'Ilwaine's Sermon, which he has since written to me, contained a garbled and unfair representation of his sentiments. The quotation here given is made from a valuable tract, in which Mr. M'Ilwaine has, himself, published the substance of his Sermons.

nervous system. It affects poor young girls who are working in factories all day, with very insufficient food, and these girls I have seen myself suffering under the complaints I shall mention. I have seen them in hysteria. I have known it to end in epilepsy. I have seen them in cata-. lepsy. I have known it to result, in many cases, in madness."

It is to be supposed that something of the same kind may have occurred in other localities also; and even where the evil stops short of actual lunacy, still the whole process of " being stricken down " is only a derangement more or less violent of the health of the body and mind. The question then arises, are we justified in producing this derangement of health; and when it terminates disastrously, are we justified in putting the matter from us as something mysterious, " which we cannot fathom;" or are we bound to inquire whether our own indiscretion, or ignorance of natural laws, may not have been the cause of the evil we deplore.

At the beginning of last winter the Archdeacon of Meath delivered a lecture at the Adelaide Hospital on the importance to clergymen of a certain amount of medical knowledge. The whole subject of his lecture (and especially that part in which he speaks of hysteria), has received important illustrations from recent events.* If those who had the management of this revival movement had been better instructed, they would have recognized in the physical manifestations which accompanied it, the symptoms of disease, and would not have been tempted to suppose them-miraculous. They are no new thing, but have occurred on many different occasions, and have often been described by medical writers. I may refer to a highly interesting article in the *Dublin Quarterly Journal of Medical Science* for 1846,

---

* Since the above was written, the Archdeacon has published his own observations on the Revival at Belfast—an account which his personal familiarity with the phenomena of hysteria makes peculiarly valuable.

(quoted lately in *Saunders' News Letter*), and from which I extract the following account of the *convulsionnaires* of France, which will sufficiently show the identity of what is taking place in Ireland now with what took place in France a hundred years ago:—

"Some remain two or three days with their eyes open, but fixed, the countenance pale, the entire body insensible and rigid as that of a corpse. The most severe tortures were applied without producing any evidence of pain. In most cases the ecstacy was not continued, but the sufferers had intermissions. In ordinary cases they generally saw, heard, and understood what was passing round them, but their souls seemed occupied in the contemplation of objects which a higher power displayed to them. This supernatural state exhibits a soul disengaged—aspiring to the highest happiness—in fact, already enjoying it. In the state of convulsion, the patients generally shewed a much higher degree of intelligence and penetration than was natural to them. Girls, who were extremely timid, of low birth and without talent, spoke under the excitement of the disease with eloquence, accuracy, and elegance, on the corruption and fall of man. A young girl, who in her ordinary state was so stupid and rude as almost to pass for an idiot, when in convulsions showed so much penetration, and answered questions so ably, that she might have passed for a person of excellent education and great natural talents."—*Carré de Montgéron, la Vérité des Miracles.*

And having given an account of many other occasions on which similar scenes took place in communities widely differing in their forms of religious belief, the medical journal, already cited, sums up the whole in the following words:—

"In considering these sad histories we cannot help reflecting on the curious circumstance, that every one of the strange and anomalous phenomena of the hysteric state were produced on a great scale. We see the propagation of the disease by sympathy; the combination of the voluntary and involuntary in the acts of the sufferers, the tendency to deceive for the purpose of exciting that sympathy, and lastly, the production of the mesmeric or magnetic phenomena as a common occurrence."

Take into consideration, now, that Scripture no where warrants us in expecting such bodily convulsions to accompany conversion. The only case in the New Testament of a man being "stricken down" was that of St. Paul; and

this was the case of a sensible miracle accompanied by light
from heaven, and by sounds, perceptible by the senses of
Paul's companions as well as his own.* In every other case
those who were converted by God's Spirit remained in full
possession of their bodily faculties. Seeing then that this

---

* This fact, that Scripture does not warrant us in expecting bodily convulsions to accompany conversion, causes much perplexity to those who
regard the prostrations in the North as God's work. For instance, a
reviewer of this Sermon is reduced to take up the Roman Catholic position,
that the fact that this method of conversion is unscriptural is no proof that
it is not apostolical. He tells us, that whether such demonstrations took
place in apostolical times as those we now hear of in the North, *we have no
means of knowing;* that although "such manifestations are not recorded
(except in one *or two* cases) in New Testament accounts of conversion,"
this is because "in the Sacred Narrative the *results* of conversions are
given, but not in most cases the accompanying demonstrations;" and he
gives a reason for admiring "the wisdom of the Divine writer in refraining
from giving particulars."

I do not think it worth my while to assail a position from which one
cannot but think that when it was seriously attacked the defender would
run away, and I simply state my belief that if anything like what is now
taking place in the North had occurred in apostolic times, we should have
read of it in the Bible.

With regard to the one case of St. Paul (for the "*or two*" I take to be
a rhetorical flourish), I add a few remarks, since this is the case relied on
by those who hold that the prostrations in the North are the effects, not of
disease, but of the immediate power of God.

I. Is it certain that St. Paul was "stricken down" at all? It is recorded
that when Paul and his fellow-travellers beheld the miraculous appearance
of a light from heaven surpassing the brightness of an Eastern sun at noon,
they *all* (Acts, xxvi. 14) fell on the ground. Now it is certain (see Lev.
ix. 24 ; Josh. v. 14 ; Judges, xiii. 20 ; 1 Chron. xxi. 16), that the first act
of Jews who should be witnesses of such a supernatural appearance, would
be to fall on their faces to the ground. With regard to Paul's companions
(whose conversion is not recorded) I believe myself that they did not fall,
because they could not help it, but that the act was the spontaneous expression of their reverence and awe. With regard to St Paul himself, I
believe that he was in no trance or swoon, but in full possession of his
faculties, that he saw the Lord Jesus with his bodily eyes (1 Cor. ix. 1,
xv. 8), and that he spoke with him in a voice audible to those about him.
In the words of Calvin, "Quamvis metu perculsus in terram ceciderit, dis-
tinctam tamen audit vocem, interrogat quisnam loquitur, responsum quod
datur percipit, quæ signa sunt mentis compositæ."

II. But though the words of the narrative do not force us to it, I see no
objection to our believing that St. Paul not merely *fell,* but *was cast* down
to the ground. It is to be noted, however, that on this supposition his
loss of bodily strength was not caused by "conviction of sin," but by a

phenomenon is *not* in accordance with what the Scriptures lead us to expect; and that it *is* in accordance with what the history of disease prepares us for, I cannot have a moment's doubt as to what cause to ascribe it.

And I firmly believe that wherever this is fully understood revival meetings could be conducted with perfect freedom from these bodily convulsions. Let it be once well known that they are *not permitted,** and they will not take place. The Archdeacon of Meath, in the lecture already quoted, defines hysteria as " the escape of emotional feeling from the control under which God provided that it should be kept by reason, will, and conscience;" in which case " that portion of the nervous system which gives expression to emotional feeling seems abandoned to the direction of

---

manifestation of the glory of God too overpowering for human faculties (see Ezek. i. 28; Dan. x. 8; Matt. xvii 6). If persons now-a-days fall to the ground like Paul, the phenomenon will be in accordance with Scripture, *if* they at the same time receive a miraculous revelation like Paul. This claim is actually made; but we can give good reasons for regarding such pretensions as a delusion. In the first place, they are not *proved* as St. Paul's claims were. The appearance to him was attested by the evidence of those who were with him, and by the coincidence of an independent revelation made about the same time to Ananias, and therefore it cannot, like modern visions, be accounted for as the result of a diseased state of mind or body. And secondly, since St. Paul was chosen to be an Apostle and a witness of the resurrection, we can see why it was necessary that he should actually see the ascended Redeemer; but to expect similar revelations to be repeated every day, implies ignorance of the place which miracles occupy in the scheme of the Christian dispensation.

* One of the most interesting tracts I have seen in connection with the present movement is a reprint (by M'Watters of Armagh, price one penny) of a Presbyterian account of the Revivals in America at the beginning of this century, to which the present Irish Revivals have a far greater resemblance than to the American Revivals of last year. From it I extract the following fact, which confirms the statement in the text :— " Persons always attacked by this affection in churches where it is encouraged, will be perfectly calm in other churches where it is discouraged, however affecting may be the service, and however great the mental excitement."

accident or temptation, without any internal power of control in the patient." It is evident what a difference it makes whether the patient comes to a meeting believing that it is likely that she will lose the power of self-control and that it is God's will that she should, or whether she is told that she *must* control herself or withdraw.

I think, then, that a clergyman would be right in letting it be distinctly understood that he considers it his first duty not to endanger the health or the sanity of his people; and that he does not regard any persons as fit subjects for his ministrations as long as their bodily health is in such a state that they cannot be spoken to on the subject of religion without losing their power of self-control. " If persons are stricken during public worship it might be well to remove them at once, not to the vestry-room, to a heated atmosphere, or amongst a number similarly acted upon, but to their own, or some neighbouring house, where in quiet and seclusion, under the care of some judicious minister or friends they may receive that treatment and consolation which their case requires."* I would even go further, and, if necessary,

---

* Extracted from a judicious letter, signed Presbyter, which appeared in *Saunders'*, July 6, and which is well worthy the reader's perusal.

As to the effects of the opposite conduct, see a letter of an eye witness, the Rev. Edward Metcalf, which appeared in the *Daily Express*, July 9. He describes several of the cases which he saw as originally nothing more than cases of fainting under excitement, but which were worked into hysterics by keeping them for two or three hours, as is the case frequently, without any of the ordinary remedies which are used in such cases being resorted to, but "instead thereof a very boisterous scene of excitement is carried on around them in exceedingly loud hymn singing and praying at the pitch of the voice."

Elsewhere he describes one of those cases :—

" A girl of about twenty years of age was leading some persons in most boisterous hymn singing round a girl, who had fainted at a meeting which had just closed, and who was evidently suffering under a hysterical affec-

advise that any persons who distrusted their power of self-control should leave the meeting; and if, notwithstanding this, "cases" occurred, I should adjourn the meeting.

In this way, I believe, that in a very short time all the "physical phase" of the movement could be suppressed, and without in the least injuring or impeding the progress of any real work of God's Spirit on the souls of the people. For, I must add, that it is in the cases where the conversion of people from a life of previous ungodliness has been accompanied by this physical prostration, that I am myself least hopeful as to the permanence of the work.

I should expect the means here recommended to be effectual, if employed in districts which the physical manifestations have not yet reached; but not so where they are prevalent, and are generally regarded as the most decisive evidences of the work of God. What is a clergyman then to do? Is he to shock the prejudices of his people, and alienate their confidence, by publicly discountenancing that in which they place most reliance,* and which some will

---

tion; but this young person resisted even the authority of the doctor, who wished to have the girl removed to near the air, and her dress loosened a little, saying that she had been a 'case,' and understood it much better, and nothing was so good as hymn singing."

I add another quotation from the letter last cited, showing the mischief done, not merely to the bodies, but to the spiritual condition of the subjects of these fits, who, supposing themselves the subject of a miracle, are led o despise the ordinary means of grace:—

" I was told by one woman to whom the doctor of this town, a most kind man, whose heart is altogether with the work, led me, that although she could neither read nor write, and although she had not known any thing before, yet now no man or minister could teach her any thing, as she had been one of the 'cases.'"

* The light in which these are regarded may be illustrated by an account of a meeting in Lurgan, given in the *Banner of Ulster*, Tuesday, July 5. "A feeling of devout attention pervaded the meeting, and *although* there

testify was the miraculous means of their own conversion?
May he not have reason to believe that the prevalent feeling
of awe, and consequent willingness to attend to religion, is
is to be traced almost exclusively to the prevalent belief
in the miraculous character of these phenomena? May he
not then shrink from assailing this belief, lest if he should
succeed in overturning it, he should also undo the good that
has resulted from it; while if he should fail, he would be
himself regarded as an opposer of the work of the Holy Spirit?
I can only answer that we must speak the truth at all
hazards. We must not accept the agency of evil to do
God's work. Rather abandon the revival work altogether
than found it on a belief in false miracles. There can be
no hope of the soundness of any work if a falsehood is at
the bottom of it. And I would say this, even if one could
not point to dangers which attend the false persuasion that
one has been the subject of these miraculous influences; the
dangers namely of ill-grounded security, of spiritual pride,
of contempt of the ordinary means of grace, and of the
ordinary ministry of the word.*

---

were no decided physical symptoms of awakening, *yet* much good was apparently done." In these districts the question now seems to be whether
those who have not passed through this process are to be regarded as
Christians, and the Bishop of Down finds it necessary to " caution his
audience against the erroneous opinion that there had been no important
influence of the Spirit—no real conversion of God—except in the cases of
conviction which had been accompanied by an external influence upon the
body."—*Ballymena Observer*, July 9.

* Since the above was written it has received a commentary in an occurrence which took place in Belfast on Sunday last. A sermon was preached
in Christ Church by the Dean of Emly, a leading " Evangelical" clergyman,
of well known gentleness of manner, and therefore most unlikely, either
by his matter or his manner, to give offence to the congregation whom he
addressed. On his teaching them, however, that sudden conversions were
not the ordinary method by which God proceeds, many of the congregation

I must not speak exclusively, however, of this "physical phase" of the revival movement. Supposing this entirely banished, I should speak of the remaining part of the work in terms, certainly not of condemnation, but of caution. Let me repeat what I said in the sermon, that the emotional part of our nature is only a part of it, and that the work of the Holy Spirit is done on the entire. I believe that it is a clergyman's duty to give his especial attention at any time to that part of his work for which the providence of God seems to open up most hopes of success; but then he should never, in exclusive attention to that part, forget that it is only a part, not the whole. Thus, for example, if in any district there seemed great readiness in the Roman Catholic population to receive information on those points on which we believe their church to be in error, the clergyman ought

---

rose, and leaving the church, adjourned to a prayer meeting conducted by one of themselves. It is not very strange that men who suppose themselves to have been the subjects of miracles should consider themselves above ordinary instruction ; but it is disheartening while we are rejoicing at one evil spirit's being cast out, to see other evil spirits entering in and taking possession.

The following additional illustrations are from the American writer already cited :—" If a minister, however evangelical in faith and practise, did not ' come fully up to the mark,' i.e., if he expressed any disapprobation, ministered any caution, attempted to correct any extravagances, he was not only set down immediately as being hostile to the Revival, but even interrupted and prevented from proceeding in his discourse, by some of the multitude, who commenced singing or praying, or exhorting or shouting, which ever was at the time found most convenient by the leaders of this wild disorder." " One general prominent feature attending this revival everywhere was the strange, mistaken disposition in a very large portion of the people to undervalue the public means of religion, and in the place thereof to promote a kind of tumultuous exercise in which themselves could take an active part, if not become the principal leaders. Hence some of these would-be leaders have been known to lie down and sleep in the time of preaching, and during some of the most serious and solemn addresses, and as soon as the sermon was over, suddenly rise to their feet and sing, and shake hands, and pray, and exhort with all the apparent energy of a saint or messenger from heaven."

thankfully to avail himself of the opening. But if after a time he appeared wholly absorbed in controversy it would surely be right to caution him—"Do not forget that the enlightenment of the intellect of your people is only a part of your work. Remember that it is one thing to make them Protestants: another to make them Christians. In vain will they have been convinced of the errors of Romanism, if their increased knowledge has not taught them to love their Saviour better, and has not made their lives more holy." So, again, if drunkenness prevailed in a parish, the clergyman would be bound to take advantage of any opportunity that presented itself for the promotion of temperance; yet he would remember that though the Gospel leads to morality, morality by itself is not the Gospel; and that it is possible a man may forsake drunkenness without being nearer to Christ.

An opportunity offers itself at the present time, in many places, of appealing with success to the emotional part of our nature; of so stirring up many from thoughtlessness, worldliness, or indolence, and bringing them to devote themselves to Christ, in a manner they have never done before. A clergyman ought surely to take advantage of such an opportunity; but then he ought not to forget that, as I said, the emotional part of our nature is only a part of it; and, as I may add, a part which lies much nearer the surface in some people than in others. Some persons can be easily moved to tears by a tale of fictitious distress, and yet may not possess as much real benevolence as others of less lively imaginations, or less excitable temperament. And in religion, the emotions may be touched, and yet the heart may not be changed, and the principles of action may remain unrenewed.

Some of my readers will, perhaps, more readily acknowledge this if they study the same phenomenon as it presents itself in communities different from our own. I have alluded in the sermon to the Jesuit religious exercises; and I might still more aptly have referred to the missions of the Redemptorist Fathers through this country, at which, I believe, scenes of excitement have taken place equalling anything that has taken place in the revivals of the North—the physical prostrations excepted. I have been told that sober-minded Roman Catholic heads of families have had scruples about exposing their wives and daughters to those scenes of excitement. The following accounts of the proceedings of similar missions are extracted from "*Meyrick's Working of the Church in Spain.*"

"As he took down the crucifix and held it out, the sobs which had been gradually increasing, burst out through the church into loud crying like that of children, while he poured out a fervent prayer, crying bitterly, for himself and for the people. I wish I could give you an idea of the effect of the scene presented by the church crowded with people, crying violently, with their faces turned up to the pulpit. There was something very striking in the words of the prayer, with which he concluded, the depth of its self-abasement, and the entire confidence and even familiarity of some of his expressions."

On another occasion he writes:—

"By this time the nerves of the people were so worked up, that they were ready to cry about anything or nothing, and at this point one woman, by my side, actually howled so as to make it difficult for me to hear.
 "How many confessions there have been cannot be told, for when once the people began to confess it was like an epidemic. The Capuchins have done their duty, and done it well; but when they are gone, and the people are left to the *despised ministrations of the ordinary* confessors, there is much danger that the majority will fall back again. For the present, the improved behaviour in the churches is striking. These are such a very excitable people, *all feelings and no principles, and have a marvellous way of combining religious feeling with the practice of sin.*"

Let those who are ready enough to grant that such dangers may exist in the case of Roman Catholics, consider that they may also exist in our own case. The excitement of emotion is neither the only, nor an infallible mark of grace. It *may* be the means by which the Holy Spirit begins a work which he will afterwards bring to perfection; or it *may* be but the natural result of constitutional susceptibility of impression; and may spend itself out without producing a single permanent result.

In conclusion, lest any should mistake the spirit in which I write, I desire to add, that the testimony I have received leaves me no room to doubt that the Revival movement in the North has been attended by the suppression of drunkenness and profanity, by general reformation of moral character; by increased interest in everything pertaining to religion; by increased attendance at public worship, and at the holy communion That this work will be permanent in every case it would be too much to expect—that it will be so in very many, I hope and believe. In a work blessed*

---

* In this third edition I desire to repeat my acknowledgment of good effected by the movement, because I fear that in England attention has been chiefly attracted by the extravagances with which it has been in some cases accompanied. Every great revolution is commonly attended with excesses, and those in proportion to the evils from which the reaction takes place. And from what I have heard on trustworthy authority of the previous deadness and absence of religion in many of the districts in which the revival has spread, I feel the less wonder that the overthrow of this indifference should be accompanied by much of which I cannot approve, and the less difficulty in believing that even where these excesses have most prevailed, there is a large preponderance on the side of good.

It is another question, however, whether we cannot have the good of this movement without the evil. And I believe none do more hinderance to the work of God than those who insist on our regarding as *His*, everything that is done by the fallible men who are labouring in His cause. I recommend to their consideration the following words of one who will not be thought indifferent to the cause of evangelical religion :—

"On the one hand precipitate and harsh condemnations of extraordinary appearances of a revival in religion, when it afterwards appears that God was eminently prospering His Gospel, by those who followed not with these rash censurers, are very common : and so on the other, is an indis-

with such good results I acknowledge the hand of God Nor shall I refuse to do so because—as must happen in any work where men are the agents and men the objects—in any work done on sinful beings by fallible beings—because mistakes and deception may have mixed themselves up with it. Many ungodly persons may have been drawn in to go through the outward process of " conviction," whose hearts have been wholly unaffected. Many may have deceived themselves by mistaking transitory emotions for real change of principle. Too sanguine clergymen may have accepted with too little caution these appearances of promise, and may have encouraged young converts, who were at best but " girding on their harness," to boast themselves as though they were putting it off. But when all deductions are made, 1 trust that much will remain, which will be to the praise and glory of the Lord on the day of His appearing.

It is then in no spirit of hostility that I have laboured to distinguish from the real work of God those human elements which in my judgment disfigure this movement. If clergymen pet and encourge what they ought to suppress, thereby inducing their people to adopt false tests of the presence of God's Spirit, and giving occasion to the enemy to blaspheme, it is a Christian duty to labour to correct these errors. *Faithful are the wounds of a friend; but the kisses of an enemy are deceitful.*

---

criminate sanctioning of all that is done or observed on these occasions, as *divine*, when the event shows, that human infirmity and depravity, and Satan's artifice, in various ways, concurred to disgrace, if possible, and stop the good work of the Holy Spirit. To wait, to examine and observe, and impartially to distinguish between what is Scriptural and what is unscriptural in these extraordinary events, and not to give an opinion till the whole be maturely weighed, so as to leave but little danger either of condemning the work of God, or of sanctioning the delusions of the devil, is a chief point of heavenly wisdom."—(*Rev. Thomas Scott's Commentary on St. Luke*, ix. 50).

POSTSCRIPT.

SINCE the above was sent to press, I have received the following communication from a clerical friend in the North, to whom I had written for information, and of whose piety, sound judgment, and sobriety of mind, I have the highest opinion. Thinking it desirable to put on record some authentic facts in the history of this movement, I have obtained his permission to print it here, omitting some things written in the confidential freedom of a private letter, not intended for publication :—

"To pronounce an opinion as to the present extraordinary religious movement of which Belfast is the centre, is by no means easy, even for one who has carefully watched it throughout, and has had many opportunities of seeing its different phases. There is as great a difference of opinion among the inhabitants of Belfast as among strangers. Even the facts are by no means easily ascertained ; I shall, however, try to give you my impressions of it as well as I can.

"Last year several clergymen went over to America, partly with a view to see the revivals there. Some of these went through the country, lecturing on the subject of revivals, and giving an account of what they had seen in America. These lectures were very numerously attended, and excited a great interest. In different parts of this county revival meetings were got up on the American plan, but were carried on for a long time without any apparent result. In some of these meetings there was much that was extravagant. The shouting, and gesticulation, and uproar, were sufficient to account for some of the results. The most sacred names and the most awful subjects were frequently and familiarly introduced. A portion of the house was separated from the rest, and called the penitential forms. To these all who were deeply affected, and who showed signs of penitence, were invited. The ministers went from one to another of the penitents, whispering in their ears, telling them to pray earnestly, shouting out texts of Scripture, and calling on the rest of the congregation to sing hymns as heartily as they could. The revival in Belfast reached its height about a month ago, when three young men, converts, were brought from Ballymena. Crowded meetings were got up for the purpose of hearing them give an account of their "conversion." They told the people of the misery which they had suffered from the conviction of sin ; and their impassioned appeals to others to follow their example, produced a very startling effect. Strong men burst into tears ; women fainted, and went off in hysterics. The piercing shrieks of those who called aloud for mercy, and the mental agony from which they suffered, were, perhaps, the most affecting that you could imagine. The penitents flung themselves on the floor, tore their hair, entreated all around to pray for them, and seemed to have the most intense conviction of their lost state in the sight of God. In some instances they were suffered to remain along with the congregation ; sometimes they were brought into the vestry, from which, however their sobs and cries were distinctly audible ; sometimes they were sent to their own homes. No one could help being strongly influenced by such scenes as these. I have seen meetings in which there was scarcely one present who was not weeping. Frequently they have been unable to close the meeting till the next day ; the persons stricken down refused to leave the place until they had found peace and comfort. Nor did these effects cease with the meeting. One woman in this neighbourhood came home, feeling that a sort of spell was over her ; a girl who had been stricken down had clasped her round the legs, and so completely frightened her that immediately on her reaching her own house she became similarly affected.

"The physical affections are of two kinds. (1) The patient either becomes deeply affected by the appeals which he or she may have heard, and bursts into the loudest and wildest exclamations of sorrow, and continues praying and pleading with God for mercy, sometimes for hours, or (2) falls down completely insensible, and continues in this state for different periods, varying from about one hour to two days. The persons affected in the latter way are chiefly females of delicate constitution— the last woman whom I saw in this state had exhausted her constitution by suckling two children at one time. The persons affected in the former way are sometimes women, frequently men. The attack comes on generally in houses of worship. I have known several cases occurring when the person attacked was engaged in his ordinary work, or when walking in the street ; but in most instances after they had attended meetings on the night before, or when their minds were deeply employed in thinking of something which they heard. In one or two instances, the patients declared that they had been awakened *out of sleep* by this state of conviction. During the continuance of the state (2) the person affected remains perfectly tranquil, apparently unconscious of everything going on around ; the hands occasionally clasped, as in prayer, the lips moving, and sometimes the eyes streaming with tears ; the pulse generally regular, and without any indications of fever. When they have recovered from this state, they sometimes speak of visions which they have seen ; sometimes they have no distinct recollection of anything which has occurred. I have known one person who has gone through this process without having attributed it to any religious feelings whatever. Generally, however, it is distinctly traceable to religious excitement, and the persons who have recovered from it represent it as the time of their ' conversion.' There is a most remarkable expression in their countenances, a perfect radiance of joy, which I have never seen on any other occasion. I would be able to single out the persons who had gone through this stage by the expression of their features. There is a very strong feeling of sympathy between those who have been affected. I have seen females rush forward to kiss each other. They express the greatest delight when their friends are visited in the same way, and frequently pray for them that they may have an attack. Some of the more ignorant of them have actually taught that no one will be saved who has not been ' converted' in the same way ; this impression has gained strength, and extended very much during the last week, and all parties, churchmen and Presbyterians are now doing everything in their power to check it.

· "The reality of the ' conversion' is supposed to be tested by ' the gift of prayer.' The converts cannot be restrained from trying their newly-found power, and I have been sometimes surprised by the appropriateness of their language. This *latter* feature, however, as we might have expected, is by no means common. They have got off by heart a few common texts of Scripture, and one or two set phrases, which they hear at the revival meetings, which they cast into the shape of a prayer. The zeal which they afterwards exhibit for the ' conversion' of their friends is most remarkable. They gather a number of their fellow-workers, whenever they have the opportunity, and read the Scriptures, and exhort and pray with them. Some of these meetings, I have been told, are most affecting. In some of the mills there have been as many as ten different prayer meetings of this sort during the intervals allowed them for breakfast and dinner. These meetings are resumed in the evening on a larger scale, generally *conducted*, (*i.e.*, presided over) by a minister of some denomination. They not unfrequently continue till twelve o'clock at night, and when the people disperse they go home in groups, singing psalms and hymns.

"I have seen a group of about fifty persons gathered round a lamp-post at one o'clock in the morning, singing psalms, and it is quite a common occurrence to meet parties in the public roads singing in the same way.

"We should very much underrate the real influence of the present movement, if we were to confine our attention to these extraordinary phenomena. I have never seen so widely spread and so deep a current of religious earnestness as pervades the *whole of society* in Belfast. At first, the Roman Catholics scoffed at it, then they were awe-stricken by it, and now they avoid all contact with Protestants as far as they can. The priests are distributing holy water, consecrated medals, and bottles of some medicinal preparation; for which they charge a price according to the circumstances of the buyer, which they tell their people will preserve them from the 'revival,' or 'the thing that's going,' as it is called.

"Among the poor Protestants the change is almost incredible. Many of the dissenting places of worship are open every evening, and nearly always full to overflowing, especially those attended by the working classes. Persons whom I have never before been able to induce to listen to any religious conversation, or to attend church, are most anxious to hear the Scriptures read and explained, and to join in prayer, and come to church. There are few poor Protestant houses where my visits are not welcomed, and people crowd after the clergyman from one house to another, wherever he may have gone. When I am walking along the streets, I am sometimes brought from house to house to see cases of 'conviction,' and to give them consolation. There is a feeling of awe pervading all classes, which renders them most anxious to listen to every word which the ministers may say, and which increases their power one hundred-fold.

"The distinguishing feature appears, however, to be the *lay* ele-

ment; the number of ignorant persons who have taken upon
themselves to teach and to pray extempore for large assemblies.
In this also, lies its chief danger. Many of these have actually
been paid at the rate of twenty shillings a-week, others have not
returned to their ordinary labour for a week or a fortnight, con-
ceiving that they have received a commission to tell what happiness they have derived from the Gospel. They are brought
from place to place; and some of their addresses on these occasions are affecting; some are very little short of blasphemous. I
have heard of one gentleman who is about to bring some of them
over to England, with a view to get up a Revival there.

"With all the excesses, however, and the risk of leading them to
suppose that religion consists in excitement, and is to be mea-
sured by the feelings, I believe that the revival has done very
great good. If we can keep up the zealous and earnest spirit
which has been created, and *teach* the many ignorant people who
have seen the value of religion, and have been startled to flee
from the wrath to come, we shall have good reason to bless God
for such an awakening.

"At the same time, I fear that other denominations will make
much more out of it than the Church. Many of the ministers of
the Church have thrown themselves into the movement with all
their souls. I myself have never done so much, as during the
last few weeks, both in the church, and in the open air, and from
house to house. I find that I have a much keener sense of the
work which is before me than I ever had before. These poor
people have shown so wonderful an appreciation of the great
doctrines of Christianity, of the heinousness of man's sin, and the
value of the Atonement, and the work of the Holy Spirit as the
Sanctifier of men's hearts, that it does one good to move among
them. But the clergy of the Church are not equal to the work
which is cast upon them. We do not suppose it to be consistent
with the principles of the Church, even though it were expedient, to give laymen the same functions which they readily
obtain in the dissenting bodies. It has become an *ordinary part*
of the public worship, in some Presbyterian and Methodist houses,
to allow the 'converts' to address the congregation, and tell
what a change has passed over them. Some of these addresses
are very solemn and affecting. I have heard instances of persons
who had been avowed sceptics, profligates, and drunkards, standing
up to tell that they had resolved to amend their lives. One
man, who had actually taken an interest in circulating sceptical
publications, told the congregation of his conversion, and went

round the several persons whom he thought he had injured by
his conversation, to try to undo the evil which he had done, as
well as he could. This is, no doubt, an extreme case, but other
persons who had been more or less careless, have made a similar
profession. Most of the persons 'stricken' had, however, been
more seriously disposed, such as Sunday-school teachers, who,
so far as we can judge, had been living a virtuous and Christian
life. The effects upon the lives of many others of those 'converts' have been in many respects remarkable. The traffic in
spirits in some parts of this county has fallen off wonderfully.
There is one place in Belfast, which is like Jude's, in Grafton-
street, Dublin, frequented by young men. It has been almost
deserted of late. Some of the worst parts of the town have presented a very different appearance since the movement began,
from what they did before. Young women who have been
'stricken,' have even thrown aside *crinoline*, and have given up
dancing and walking on Sundays.

"The whole aspect of the revivals is *puritanical ;* the chief
agency, the laity ; the most popular mode of worship, extempore
prayer. This being so, it is evident that the other denominations
are better able to throw themselve into it than the Church. If
it should lead to some plan whereby laymen, under certain con-
ditions, could be more closely incorporated with the organization
of the Church, it would be a great blessing. In confirmation
of this opinion, it is to be noticed that the services of the
Church are less popular than dissenting sereices, although in
some instances here the clergy deviated from the usual form
of evening service, by using the litany only, and having a
sermon afterwards. On Sundays our attendance is large, and
on Sunday last we had almost treble the ordinary number at the
Communion. Perhaps, when the excitement has subsided, the
Church may appear to the greater advantage, when the sobriety
of her services, and the superior education of her clergy is con-
trasted with the scenes which have been recently enacted in
other places, and the extravagant addresses they have heard.*

---

* I own that this last is the impression which my correspondent's communication produces on me. However I may have felt at other times that
greater elasticity in the Church's rules would be desirable, I must confess
my belief that but for this very want of elasticity all order would have been
swept away in the excitement that has prevailed in the North, and that
many of our churches would have exhibited such scenes of extravagance
as have appeared in some of the places of worship of every other deno-

" A good deal of what would appear to us very indecent, and well-nigh blasphemous, is simply in their case, want of taste. It is surprising that the extravagant familiarity with the most awful subjects does not destroy all their feelings of reverence. It does not produce in the minds of the poor what would be the inevitable effect with more cultivated minds."

I add some extracts from a later letter from the same correspondent, dated August 12.

"The good results of the movement are still conspicuous. I have known very few cases of persons who, in the beginning of the movement, were said to have been converted, and have since fallen away. Up to the *present* time I should say that the good has very much predominated over the evil results. There is still a very general seriousness in all circles, and much anxiety on the subject of religion ; but, at the same time, there is the utmost need of caution and firmness in repressing the undoubted mischief that has sprung up along with it.

" There are still some persons ' stricken,' but few *new* cases. They are generally persons who had been affected before in the way which I have described. It is a common thing for such persons either to predict that they will be taken ill at a particular time (naming the hour), that they will continue speechless for a certain period, and that at another definite hour they will recover their speech. During this swoon or cataleptic fit they are sometimes deaf, dumb, and blind : sometimes they are apparently dumb and blind, but still able to hear. I have seen cases of this sort in which I believe that the patients had lost all consciousness ; but in far the greater number they were able to hear, and, I believe, able to speak. I do not think that it is necessary to suppose that such persons are always impostors. It would appear rather that having sunk under great nervous exhaustion it is a painful effort to speak ; and so they do not try to speak, and at length persuade themselves that they are not able to speak. Having also been led to believe that these fits have something to do with religion, so far from struggling against them they give

---

mination that has participated in the movement. No doubt the Church would gain over many dissenters if she allowed all persons who pleased, educated or uneducated, children or adults, to conduct public prayer, and to take on themselves the office of teacher. For nothing less than this is what the present excitement has forced dissenting bodies to permit.

way to them and encourage them, under the impression that it
will be good to have passed through them. Even independently
of this impression there is also the greatest interest created in the
whole neighbourhood when it is known that there has been 'a
case;' persons gather into the house, and come in crowds about the
door. The number of strangers who have flocked into Belfast
from all parts of the country to see the revivals, chiefly to see
such extraordinary cases as these, who go away disappointed if
they should not see some person 'stricken,' supplies a constant
stream of visitors. Since the patient, the friends, the neighbours,
and in most cases, the visitors, are all predisposed to look for
something miraculous, it is no easy matter to shew that it can all
be accounted for by natural causes ; and that it is a disease to
be greatly dreaded, instead of being a direct manifestation of the
Spirit of God. A few days ago I was called on to see a young
man, whom I had known very well, who had been taken ill.
When I went into the room I found it full—some persons were
even sitting on the bed. They had been singing and praying
with him. He had got a piece of paper, on which he was writing
and answering such questions as might be put to him. He had
told them that he would continue dumb until ten o'clock the
next morning. He was manifestly extremely weak. I remon-
strated with his mother on the great impropriety of allowing so
many persons to be in the room, and succeeded in getting rid of
some of them. I told her to give her son perfect quiet, and
suggested medical advice, and explained to her what I believed
to be the real cause of the disease, and the best mode of treatment ; at the same time warning her very solemnly of the great
error of supposing that this disease was in any way connected
with the work of the Holy Spirit. I strove to convince the persons present, that the young man could speak, if he were to make
the effort. I asked him try to speak, to move his lips as he
would do if he were able to speak, so as to show us all that he
was really dumb. This he would not do. I then told them that
I believed that he could speak, as was evident from his refusal
even to make the effort. In order to show this more satis-
factorily I went over to the bed and strove to tickle him under
the arms. He kept his arms closely pressed to his side, and I
was not able to make him laugh, though a smile stole over his
face two or three times. During the whole of this time I could
see that the spectators were very much displeased ; and I believe
that if I had not known them all very well, they would have
forcibly prevented me from making any attempt to undeceive

them. As it was, they warned me of the unpopularity which would be sure to follow my attempts to interfere with what they considered a good work. Some of them were satisfied with my explanation, and have seen the mischief arising from such scenes ; but others are still under the impression that I was quenching the Spirit. But it is when the hour comes, which has been fixed for the return of the power of speech that we see the worst part of the delusion. The patients expect that their friends will then attend (one person expressed herself much displeased because the clergyman did not think proper to encourage the delusion by going to see her at the time named). There is frequently a clock in the house, and , if not, they can guess the hour by the assembling of the neighbours, who have had notice of it by the other inmates going to or coming from their work, or by some casual remark which they manage to over-hear. They generally break silence by giving some advice, or quoting a text of Scripture, or telling of a vision which they have seen, or delivering an exhortation. They sometimes go so far as to deliver messages to individuals from Christ. One of them said to a friend, at his bed-side, that the Lord had been pleased with him, but was not satisfied with his brother John. John was, for some time, greatly distressed by this supposed revelation."

I give some additional notes from the *Ballymena Observer* of July 9, several columns of which are devoted to the progress of the revival, and from a Pamphlet by Rev. Samuel Moore, a Presbyterian clergyman of Ballymena, who has taken a leading part in this work. The former extracts are marked *B. ;* the latter *M*.

Progress of the Revival.—" The largest number of ' convictions ' ever heretofore recorded as having taken place at any public assemblage of the people in this neighbourhood, occured at an open air sermon in Cullybackey, on Sunday last. On that day the Rev. Hugh Hanna, of Belfast, delivered a most powerful and soul-searching discourse, before an audience numbering above 8,000. The services of the day resulted in 116 cases of public and impulsive penitence ; besides numerous others which occurred in the course of the same evening whilst the people were proceeding on the way to their respective homes."—*B.*

" The village was full of souls wounded by the hand of God. Along the roads, in all directions, were groups encountered here and there, comforting smitten souls, or rejoicing with others that had found peace in Jesus."—*B.*

BERRY-STREET CHURCH.—"The number of 'manifested convictions' during the progress of the services was forty-two. But this number must be considerably increased if we add all those who, as is usual, are overtaken on arriving at their homes.

"The arrows of the Lord are shot into the minds of the people, and bring many down at the instant; others bear up against their wounds for a time, but surrender to the Lord at last."—*B.*

It is not to be supposed, however, that these convictions were all new cases. It is not uncommon for the same person to be "convicted" fifteen or twenty times; nor do these convictions always terminate favourably. though they are described as generally doing so.

Alternation of Sin and Conviction.—"Some are frequently convicted though they do not return to their old ways; perhaps to intensify the work. Conviction and sinning alternate with some; and ultimately the conviction seems in the mean time to cease, and the sins remain; while in other cases the very reverse is the result."—*M.*

Dangerous aspect of three Cases.—"The minds of some three poor creatures have given way, whether from predisposition or fright, or the long-continued apprehension of hell, without any feeling or hope of deliverence; or whether from injudicious treatment, or *cruel restraint from the society and sympathy of kindred spirits,* or from want of food and sleep; or from several of these causes combining, I am unable to determine. The first of these is now quite well and spiritually happy; the second is in the asylum, slowly improving; the third died. I visited the second of these cases, and, amid all her frenzy, and wild and maniac wanderings, at intervals she held firm by Christ. Some one said to her, that I had come to see her. She wildly, *yet perhaps wisely* replied, 'Mr. Moore, Mr. Moore! I don't want him. Let him go to them that sent for him. He can do me no good. Jesus Christ alone can hold me.' She thought she was pulled out of the 'horrible pit,' as she called it, that she was still on the very edge of it, held out of it only by the hand of Jesus; and her apprehension was that He would let her go."—*M.*

Convictions not invariably accompanied with Knowledge.—"One person, rather advanced in years, quite uneducated, suffered during a whole night, bodily prostration and pain, and felt darkness over her mind. In the morning she was impressed that she was a sinner, and was anxious about her soul, but knew nothing whatever, or, at least, could tell nothing about the Saviour. She seemed to me made ready for apostolical instruction."—*M.*

Superiority of Converts to Earthly Affections.—" I saw a mother on her knees, her eyes raised heavenward, her hands energetically clasped. She often smiled, but, perhaps for an hour, she did not speak. One of her children, some two years old, was injudiciously allowed to come into the apartment. On seeing its mother it raised a crying as if it was being murdered. . Her eye never twinkled, nor did a muscle of her face move. She remained stationary, statue-like, absorbed in the object of her adoration. Yes so it must be. Oblivion's wave must swell over the mind of the redeemed parent, sweeping thence all remembrance of the child once dearly loved, now irremediably lost ; or there must be such a perfect sympathy with the heart of the Holy Jesus as to necessitate a cordial hatred to all that is hostile and hurtful to Him ; or, as in this case, the soul must be so absorbed in contemplating, adoring the Redeemer, that no distraction of thought or feeling to an alien object will be possible." —*M.**

Exclusive Character of the Love of Converts for each other.— " The converts feel and manifest intense love for each other. In fact they cannot be happy out of each other's society. They don't care very much for any one, though a Christian, who has not their towering love and zeal ; but any one whom they consider to be one of themselves, ' a brother ' or ' a sister,' as they say, they will receive with open arms."—*M.*

Employment of Children as Preachers.—" The good people statedly worshipping in Great George's-street Church, Belfast, with many earnest men who joined them from evening to evening had been long earnestly praying for, and expecting, an outpouring of the Holy Spirit. They had reason to believe that some good was being accomplished, and souls saved at their meeting for

---

* The Archdeacon of Meath might possibly give a different explanation of this case. He says :—" There is one perversion of moral feeling which always exists in hysteria, and more than anything else might make us doubt whether hysteria be chosen of God as a means of conversion, and that is—selfishness. The woman who *habitually indulges* hysterical feeling, as many in Belfast are now taught to indulge it, becomes the most selfish and unsympathetic being in the world.'

prayer ; but it was only within the last few days that an abundant portion of the Spirit was bestowed upon them* They are now, however, rejoicing over many 'convictions'; and it is to be hoped they will yet have cause for greater joy over many conversions. In such a crowded house, and with so many 'visible manifestations,' it would be impossible to preserve that order and decorum so becoming the house of God. *It would be as well in future to prevent any small boys and girls from addressing a crowded audience* like that which assembles from evening to evening in this church; and that the assembly should be dismissed at a reasonable hour of the evening, as in most instances, late and protracted meetings are productive of evil rather than good. It would, besides, be well to take those parties home at once who have been deeply affected. In one place of worship at least, arrangements have been made, whereby they are taken home at once, and one, or perhaps two Christian men or women sent with them to give such directions to their thoughts, and such comfort as may be found necessary. The consequence is, in general, found to be that at the most crowded assemblages, every one gets home by half-past ten, or latest, eleven o'clock ; and there is no confusion or unnecessary excitement."—*B.*

Converts the recipients of immediate Revelation, equal to that given to the Apostles.—"Then the views which many of the converts have of Christ, their souls being enlightened and allured to Him, how clear—how glorious !—in some cases quite as glorious as that enjoyed by the Apostle John."—(Rev. i. 13-16). —*M.*

Miraculous phase of the Movement.—The extract with which I conclude, is inserted, not because of anything extraordinary in the facts related, which will appear novel to no one who has been a witness of an exhibition of mesmeric clairvoyance. In fact, a mesmerist, accustomed with bandaged eyes to read shut books, or to read mottoes inserted in carefully closed nuts, would rather look down on an exhibition where the performer only drew her finger along the lines without reading them. One controversy being enough at a time, I express no opinion how the wonders of

---

* This means that it was only within the last few days that cases of physical prostration occurred.

mesmerism are to be accounted for, but the Ballymena Mary and
Miss Martineau's Jane, evidently belong to the same class, and if
the performances of the one can be explained without the hypo-
thesis of a miracle, so, I suppose, can those of the other. But I
have made these quotations to show how even educated persons
are infected with this craving for miracle, a craving naturally
produced by the prevalent belief that every person "stricken"
is prostrated by the miraculous agency of God. I believe that if
speedy exertions are not made, this revival, from which so many
are hoping good, will terminate to permanent delusions akin to
those of Irvingism, if not even worse.

" From our memoranda of cases wherein strong mental convictions have been accompanied by new and mysterious operations
upon the physical condition of the parties affected, we submit
the following record of phenomena, as brought under our special
notice on the evening of Saturday last. There is not a shadow
of doubt as to the facts ; and, if they are capable of explanation
upon natural principles, we must leave their elucidation to the
ingenuity of more profound philosophers. The party to whom
we refer is a young and healthy woman, but utterly uneducated—
unacquainted even with the letters of the alphabet, and heretofore unrestrained by any intelligent sense of her religious duties.
She is a servant in the house of a pious and respectable farmer,
who is an elder in one of the Presbyterian churches of Ballymena, and resident in a neighbouring district. In references
like the present we do not publish the names or initials of any
party ; but, for the sake of distinction, we shall call this woman
' Mary'—her real name, and that of every other individual heretofore referred to in these notices, we can readily supply. On
the first Sabbath of June last, Mary was severely and very pro-
perly rebuked, by a member of her master's family, for indulgence in a vicious habit of profane swearing ; on which occasion
she jeeringly replied that she would attend at a prayer meeting,
appointed to be held on a neighbouring farm that evening, and
' get the revival.' She did attend the meeting. It is to be feared
that she went only to mock—but she ' remained to pray.' In
the course of the services, conviction fell upon her soul with the
force and velocity of a thunderbolt. A shock, like that produced
by electricity, thrilled every nerve ; and, yielding to an irresis-

tible impulse, she loudly and earnestly called for heaven's mercy.
She returned to her master's house in agonies of penitence. Her
'conviction' of sin had not been succeeded by any real conversion to 'newness of life'—*for** she had no consciousness of pardon,
or any feeling that she was at peace with God. In this unhappy •
state of mental anxiety she remained till the 23rd ult., on the
evening of which day, and in a spirit of becoming seriousness,
she attended at another prayer meeting at Ballycloughan. A
similar result ensued. She was prostrated as before, and was
brought back in a state of very great excitement, but unable to
articulate a single word. The scene which then ensued took
place in the presence of her master, and in that of many other
witnesses, who are all ready to confirm the statement, if need be,
upon their sworn testimony. For some minutes Mary remained
in a standing position, but apparently unconscious of surround-
ing objects. Several times she struck the floor violently with
her feet, and raised her arms towards heaven in an imploring attitude—but she remained speechless. After a while she became
less agitated, and sunk backward into a reclining position, her
eyes firmly closed, except at brief intervals, when they were found
to be directed upward, in a gaze of fixed intensity. While in this
attitude, one of the persons present put into her hand a copy of
the New Testament. She grasped it with great eagerness, held
it upward at the full stretch of her arm, and afterwards pressed
it closely with both hands upon her breast. Now, it must be
remembered that the poor girl is utterly unable to read ; and, up
to the present moment, cannot distinguish between the right and
wrong position of any printed book. After some time she extended her arms at full length upon her lap, and opened the
Testament, her face being all the while turned upward, and her
eyes perfectly closed. In this attitude she turned over the pages,
as if in search of some particular passage of Scripture ; and,
having apparently succeeded, she deliberately commenced with the
first line of the 14th chapter of the Gospel according to St. John
—"Let not your heart be troubled, &c. ;" and slowly, as if in
reading time, she traced with the point of her finger, but without
sight of eye, or motion of the lip, every word of that chapter—
ending precisely with the concluding line.† She then, to the

---

* Note the test here applied of conversion to newness of life.
† It is not necessary to know how to read in order to be able to distinguish where a chapter of the New Testament begins and ends.

astonishment of all present, deliberately marked that portion of the Gospel record, by folding in the leaf in such a manner that its point precisely corresponded with the commencement of the chapter. She then apparently renewed her search for other passages elsewhere in the Testament ; and she did not cease her examination of the book until seemingly at peace of mind, and thoroughly satisfied with the investigation. In this way she fixed upon twenty-three portions of the sacred volume—running her finger slowly along the selected lines, which were sometimes comprised within a single sentence, and in other places extended to two or three verses. In every case she deliberately marked each passage by carefully turning down, folding, or rolling in the upper corner of the leaf, in such a manner that it invariably pointed, with perfect accuracy, to the figures denoting the verse or verses which she had apparently studied ! This solemn scene lasted for a period of about five hours ; and its effect upon the awe-stricken by-standers (Mary being well known to every one of them) may be readily conceived. Her master occasionally led the assemblage in appropriate prayer, and all present were affected to tears. The book, with every mark in it precisely as made by the girl's own hand, was secured by Mary's master upon the spot. It is before us at the present moment. We have examined it with great care ; and, from that inspection, we are enabled to state that the marked passages bear, with pointed accuracy, upon the Gospel plan for the redemption of our fallen race, and the restoration of peace and hope to the believing Christian. Every passage, as traced and marked by the seemingly unconscious girl, was read by her master before all present, for which purpose the book was repeatedly taken from her hands, and again restored to her ; and it is worthy of remark that, when it happened to be presented to her with the leaves inverted, she invariably restored the volume to its proper position. Another occurrence, in connexion with the phenomena, excited intense surprise and bewilderment among the by-standers. On one occasion, after Mary had paused in the usual manner, and traced the lines of some particular portion of the Gospel, her master removed the book, and read the passage aloud, without observing that she *had not marked the verse.* The volume was then returned to her, *closed.* She opened it immediately, her hands trembling with manifest agitation, and turning over the leaves, as if in anxious search for something which she had lost, she directly found, re-traced, and carefully marked the *identical verse* which her master had just read ! At another time, after she had traced a passage, and was apparently pondering upon the contents, her master removed the book, read the portion which she had traced, and then *marked it himself.* On regaining possession of the volume, Mary became somewhat excited. She searched for her master's mark, found it, erased it carefully by unfolding the corner of the leaf—which she then pressed with her finger in repeated efforts to smooth away the crease. Not satisfied with that, she raised a portion of her gown, and passed it repeatedly over the entire surface of the leaf, as if with an anxious desire to obliterate the mark effectually! In this mysterious state of mind and body, the girl remained from ten o'clock at night till half-past three on the following morning. On regaining her natural condition she had no distinct recollection of anything that had occurred from the time of her prostration at the prayer meeting—except a strong and still remaining impression that she had been tempted by the Evil One, or by her own evil heart, to unbelief; and that she had found help, defence, sustaining grace, and perfect consolation, within the sacred volume. We repeat our assurance, that there is not the shadow of a doubt as to the facts of this case. Can medical science or intellectual philosophy explain the phenomena? Any suggestion of imposition on the part of Mary must be silenced by the unquestionable fact that she does not know a single letter of the alphabet;* and we have only to add that, by every witness of the occurrence, the guiding power—the temporary illumination of mind—is attributed to the agency of the Holy Spirit.

" Another new and astonishing phase of the prevailing influence has become developed in the course of the present week in the case of a girl of pious and exemplary character, now thirteen years of age, and resident in Ballymena. She was 'impressed' for the first time about a month ago, and has since enjoyed great tranquillity of spirit, and good ordinary health, subject, however, to brief intervals of sudden weakness of body, accompanied by silent, but very evident ecstasy of the mind. On Saturday last, whilst in progress of recovery from one of these visitations, it was discovered that she had become totally dumb. Her tongue was paralysed; and, although otherwise quite well, she remained entirely without power of speech. In the course of that day she wrote the following words with a pencil upon a sheet of paper, and delivered it to her parents :—' I will recover my speech on Tuesday at four o'clock, and lose it again on Wednesday at ten

---

* And by the account of Mary's previous character, given at the commencement.

o'clock. An angel told me so to-day. 2nd July, 1859.'* We visited the girl at her father's house at half-past three o'clock on Tuesday. She was then quite well, but quite speechless. The written document was submitted for our inspection, and the above is a true copy of it. The point of the girl's tongue appeared to be turned downwards; there was a hollow curve along the centre of the entire surface; and it had been examined on the previous day by a respectable physician of the town. About a quarter before four o'clock, a weakness gradually crept over the poor girl, and within a few minutes she was found to be in a state of nerveless stupor. *Precisely at four o'clock*, and while yet in her apparently unconscious state, she suddenly regained the power of speech; and, to the astonishment of all present, exercised it in an outburst of sacred melody—clear, solemn, and harmonious. Her first words were those of the hymn, commencing thus:—

> ' I will arise and go to Jesus,
> He will embrace me in His arms;'

and she appeared to be fully awake before she had concluded the singing of the first verse! During the remainder of the evening she expressed herself as quite happy, spoke fluently, and was repeatedly engaged in prayer. About half an hour before midnight, she became instantaneously and totally blind! Soon afterwards, and while persons were engaged in singing hymns with her, she suddenly exclaimed,—'Hush.' She appeared to be listening intently for a moment; and immediately afterwards explained that she had heard a voice which desired her to be comforted, 'for she would be restored to sight before being again deprived of speech.' The prediction was verified. Her eyes were opened at half-past nine on the following morning, and after another weak interval, she became speechless for the second time, *precisely at ten o'clock*, and remained so till two o'clock in the afternoon of same day! Soon after that hour we paid her a second visit, and found her in a state of much bodily weakness—apparently unconscious of any object within view, but with an expression of countenance denoting perfect tranquillity of heart and soul. She was surrounded by deeply affected relatives; and, during our stay, she neither spoke to, nor was addressed by, any individual present. While in this very extraordinary condition she sung, softly,

---

* Predictions of this kind are also ordinary mesmeric phenomena.

sweetly, and with perfect accuracy, an entire hymn, one verse
of which we noted as follows :—

> ' The way to heaven is straight and plain;
>   Will you go ?
> Repent, believe, be born again ;
>   Will you go ?
> The Saviour cries aloud to thee,
> ' Take up thy cross and follow me,
> And thou shalt my salvation see ;
>   Will you go ?' '

"We shall only add that on every point of reference to the
above mysterious occurrences, we have been careful to state
nothing but facts—facts well known to hundreds of the population. Who will explain them ?"

The newspapers have since contained accounts of other even
more successful exhibitions of both the kinds described in the
foregoing extract. I have heard also of one girl, who seems to
have been counterfeiting something like the *stigmata* of St.
Francis. She shewed the mark of cross on her breast, which
she said no washing could obliterate. The stimulus under which
such exhibitions are got up are described in a letter from the
correspondent to whom I am already so largely indebted. "There
has been an enormous influx of visitors from all parts of the
world, who have sometimes shown even less prudence than the
wildest of our native celebrities. They have come to see some
strange thing, and are not satisfied to go away with their wishes
ungratified. So there is a constant *demand* for every form of
extravagance, and in such a population as ours, with a large
number of poor, uneducated cunning workers, there is no difficulty in keeping up the *supply*. Because the visitors, coming
with the feelings natural to persons bent on sight-seeing, are
very willing to *pay* for the value which they receive. A tale of
distress, *very often real*, very often fictitious, appeals strongly to
their feelings, and they are expected to contribute towards its
relief. The more wonderful is the tale, the greater it is supposed will be the contribution, the larger the number of visitors.
The appetite for the marvellous has grown with what it fed on.
Many persons of the middle classes of more than ordinary intelligence and education, are willing to believe the most absurd
stories without putting them to the slightest test."

I regret that want of space compels me to omit several interesting illustrations of them with which my correspondent has
furnished me.